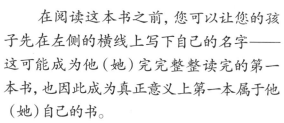

亲爱的爸爸妈妈们：

在阅读这本书之前，您可以让您的孩子先在左侧的横线上写下自己的名字——这可能成为他（她）完完整整读完的第一本书，也因此成为真正意义上第一本属于他（她）自己的书。

作为美国最知名的儿童启蒙阅读丛书"I Can Read!"中的一册，它专为刚开始阅读起步的孩子量身打造，具有用词简单、句子简短、适当重复，以及注重语言的韵律和节奏等特点。这些特点非常有助于孩子对语言的学习，不论是学习母语，还是学习作为第二语言的英语。

故事的主角是鼎鼎大名的贝贝熊一家，这一风靡美国近半个世纪的形象对孩子具有天然的亲和力，很多跟贝贝熊有关的故事都为孩子所津津乐道。作为双语读物，它不但能引导孩子独立捧起书本，去了解书中有趣的情节，还能做到真正从兴趣出发，让孩子领略到英语学习的乐趣。

就从贝贝熊开始，让您的孩子爱上阅读，帮助他们开启自己的双语阅读之旅吧！

图书在版编目（CIP）数据

许愿星：英汉对照 / （美）博丹（Berenstain, J.），（美）博丹（Berenstain, M.）著；姚雁青译. —乌鲁木齐：新疆青少年出版社，2013.1

（贝贝熊系列丛书）

ISBN 978-7-5515-2734-7

Ⅰ.①许… Ⅱ.①博… ②博… ③姚… Ⅲ.①英语－汉语－对照读物②儿童故事－美国－现代 Ⅳ.①H319.4：I

中国版本图书馆CIP数据核字(2012)第273212号

版权登记：图字 29-2012-24

The Berenstain Bears and the Wishing Star

copyright©2005 by Berenstain Bears, Inc.

This edition arranged with Sterling Lord Literistic, Inc.

through Andrew Nurnberg Associates International Limited

贝贝熊系列丛书

许愿星

（美）斯坦·博丹　简·博丹　绘著　Stan & Jan Berenstain　　姚雁青　译

出 版 人	徐 江	策 　 划	许国萍
责任编辑	贺艳华	美术编辑	查 璇　刘小珍
法律顾问	钟 　麟　13201203567（新疆国法律师事务所）		

新疆青少年出版社

（地址：乌鲁木齐市北京北路29号　邮编：830012）

Http://www.qingshao.net　　E-mail：QSbeijing@hotmail.com

印 　刷	北京时尚印佳彩色印刷有限公司	经 　销	全国新华书店
开 　本	787mm×1092mm　 1/16	印 　张	2
版 　次	2013年1月第1版	印 　次	2013年1月第1次印刷
印 　数	1-10000册	定 　价	9.00元
标准书号	ISBN 978-7-5515-2734-7		

制售盗版必究　举报查实奖励:0991-7833932　　版权保护办公室举报电话：0991-7833927

销售热线:010-84853493 84851485　　如有印刷装订质量问题 印刷厂负责掉换

The Berenstain Bears

I Can Read!

and the
WISHING STAR
许愿星

(美) 斯坦·博丹 简·博丹 绘著
Stan & Jan Berenstain

姚雁青 译

CHISO 新疆青少年出版社

One day the Bear family went to the mall.
They passed the toy store.
They looked in the toy store window.
"What a beautiful teddy bear!" said Sister.

一天，贝贝熊一家去逛商场。
他们经过一家玩具店。
他们朝着玩具店的橱窗里看。
"好漂亮的泰迪熊啊！"小熊妹妹羡慕地说。

"It's okay," said Brother.
"If you like teddies."
"Well, I do," said Sister, "and I *love* that teddy."

"如果你是泰迪迷，那它还算不错吧。"小熊哥哥评论道。
"我当然是泰迪迷，而且我很喜欢那只泰迪熊。"小熊妹妹回答。

Hmm, thought Papa,
Sister's birthday is coming.
Mama had the same thought.

"嗯，"熊爸爸想，"小熊妹妹的生日就快到了呀。"
熊妈妈也在想同样的事。

6

That night the cubs were doing their homework.

Brother was making a map of Bear Country.

Sister was doing numbers homework.

She was not doing well with numbers.

She got a C on her last report card.

Papa was helping her.

She wanted to get a B or even an A.

那天晚上，小熊们都在做作业，

小熊哥哥在画一张熊王国的地图，

小熊妹妹在做算术作业。

她算术不是很好，

最近的一次测验只得了个"C"。

熊爸爸正在教她。

她很想得到一个"B"，

如果能得"A"当然就更好啦！

Soon it was bedtime.
"Look!" said Mama.
"The wishing star."

时间过得飞快，小熊们该上床睡觉了。
"看哪，许愿星！"熊妈妈喊道。

"What is the wishing star?" asked Sister.
"It is the first star that comes
out at night," said Mama.
"You can wish upon it."

"许愿星是什么？" 小熊妹妹问。
"到了晚上，天空中亮起来的第一颗星星就是许愿星，"
熊妈妈回答，"你可以对着它许愿。"

Then Mama said the wishing star rhyme:
"Star light, star bright,
first star I see tonight.
I wish I may, I wish I might
have the wish I wish tonight."

熊妈妈哼起了许愿星的歌谣：
 "星星，星星，亮晶晶，
第一颗闪亮的小星星。
我希望我能，我希望我会，
实现我今晚的愿望。"

"What happens then?" asked Sister.
"If you wish hard," said Mama,
"and you do not tell anyone your wish,
it *might* come true."

"然后呢？"小熊妹妹好奇地问。
"如果你很认真地许愿，而且不对任何人讲你许了什么愿，
这个愿望也许就会实现。"熊妈妈神秘地说。

11

"I'm going to try it," said Sister.
She said the rhyme:
"Star light, star bright,
first star I see tonight.
I wish I may, I wish I might
have the wish I wish tonight."

"好啊，我要试试看！"小熊妹妹说。
她唱起了歌谣：
"星星，星星，亮晶晶，
第一颗闪亮的小星星。
我希望我能，我希望我会，
实现我今晚的愿望。"

Then Sister fell asleep.
She dreamed of the beautiful teddy.

小熊妹妹睡着了，
她梦到了橱窗里那只漂亮的泰迪熊。

Sister's birthday came.

She got the teddy for her birthday.

"I got my wish! I got my wish!" she cried.

小熊妹妹的生日到了。

她的生日礼物真的是那只泰迪熊。

"我的愿望实现了！我的愿望实现了！"她兴奋地大喊。

14

After supper and birthday cake,
Sister and Brother did their homework.
Brother was still working on his map.
Sister was still working on numbers.
Getting a B or even an A would be so nice,
she thought.

吃完晚饭，吃完生日蛋糕，
小熊妹妹和小熊哥哥开始做作业。
小熊哥哥还在画那张地图。
小熊妹妹还在做算术题。
"要是我能得个'B'，或者得个'A'，
那该多好啊！"她想。

That night Sister made another wish.
She said the wishing rhyme again.

那天晚上，小熊妹妹对着许愿星许下了另一个愿望。
她又唱起了许愿星的歌谣。

Then she fell asleep and dreamed.
She dreamed about getting a B or even an A.

然后，她睡着了，还做了一个梦。
她梦见自己得了一个"B"，甚至还有"A"！

Sister got her report card the next day.

She got an A for numbers.

"I got my wish! I got my wish!" she cried.

第二天，小熊妹妹拿到了成绩单。

她的算术成绩是"A"。

"我的愿望实现了！我的愿望实现了！"她高兴地大喊。

Brother got a good report card, too.
They got a reward.
They were allowed to stay up
and watch a special TV show.

小熊哥哥的成绩也很棒。
他们得到了奖励——
可以晚睡觉，还可以看一个很特别的电视节目。

It was about a pony—
a beautiful, white pony.
Sister fell in love with that pony.

节目演的是一匹小马驹的故事，
那是一匹白色的小马驹，漂亮极了。
小熊妹妹立刻爱上了它。

20

That night she said the wishing rhyme again:
"Star light, star bright,
first star I see tonight.
I wish I may, I wish I might
have the wish I wish tonight."

那天晚上，她又哼起了许愿星的歌谣：
"星星，星星，亮晶晶，
第一颗闪亮的小星星。
我希望我能，我希望我会，
实现我今晚的愿望。"

Then she went to sleep and dreamed.
She dreamed about the beautiful pony.

然后，她上床睡觉，还做了一个梦。
她梦见了那匹漂亮的小马驹。

The next morning
she woke up early.
She ran downstairs.

第二天，小熊妹妹醒得特别早。
她马上跑下楼。

She ran outside to look for her new pony.

她跑到门外去找梦中的小马驹。

She looked all over.
It wasn't tied to the fence.

她到处找啊找。
小马驹没有被拴在篱笆上。

It wasn't in the shed.

小马驹没有躲在牲口棚里。

It wasn't anywhere.

到处都没有小马驹的影子。

Sister was very sad when she came back.
"What's the matter?" asked Brother.
"I did not get my wish," said Sister.
"What did you wish for?" asked Brother.
"I'm not supposed to tell," said Sister.
"You can tell if you don't
get your wish," said Brother.

小熊妹妹垂头丧气地回到家。
"你怎么啦？"小熊哥哥问。
"我没有实现我的愿望。"小熊妹妹很伤心。
"你的愿望是什么呢？"小熊哥哥又问。
"我不能说出来。"小熊妹妹回答。
"如果愿望没有实现，就可以说出来。"小熊哥哥安慰妹妹。

27

"I wished for a beautiful, white pony,"
Sister said.

"我想要那匹漂亮的白色小马驹。"
小熊妹妹委屈地说。

"Oh," said Brother."You know, Sis,
you have to be careful with the wishing star.
If you are greedy or ask for too much,
the wishing star may not hear you."

"原来如此！"小熊哥哥说，"妹妹，你可不能随随便便就许愿呀。
如果你太贪心，要的东西太多，许愿星可能就听不见你的愿望了。"

"I got my first wish," said Sister.
"It was your birthday," Brother said.
"I got my second wish," said Sister.

"我的第一个愿望实现了呀。"小熊妹妹说。
"那是因为你的生日到了。"小熊哥哥回答。
"我的第二个愿望也实现了呀。"小熊妹妹说。

"You worked hard for that A," said Brother, "but a pony? I don't know about that, Sis."

"那是因为你很用功。"小熊哥哥说,"但是那匹小马驹……我也不知道是怎么回事,妹妹。"

Sister thought about that.

Then she smiled and said,

"Well, anyway, two out of three isn't bad."

小熊妹妹想了想。

然后她笑了起来，说：

"好吧，不管怎么样，三局两胜——结果还不错呢。"